Picture the Sky

BARBARA REID

North Winds Press
An imprint of Scholastic Canada Ltd.

*With thanks to artists — for what they see,
and how they share it.*

B.R.

The illustrations for this book were made with modelling clay that was shaped and pressed onto illustration board.

Photography by Ian Crysler.

Library and Archives Canada Cataloguing in Publication

Reid, Barbara, 1957-, author, illustrator
Picture the sky / Barbara Reid.
ISBN 978-1-4431-6302-6 (hardcover)

1. Sky--Juvenile literature. I. Title.

QC863.5.R45 2017   j551.5   C2017-901620-2

www.scholastic.ca

6 5 4 3 2 1   Printed in Canada 114   17 18 19 20 21 22

There is more than one
way to picture the sky.

It can be a blanket,
or the curtain rising
on your day.

The sky can be an eyeful.

5

It can slip into
the background.

You can find it up,
down, or all around.

It can be a playground,
a highway, a home.

You can watch the passing parade.

12

You may find a story
in the sky,

or a weather report.

15

Did dinosaurs read the sky?

Can snowmen?

Can you?

There may be a sky
in your mind's eye.

Sometimes it's movie night.

The sky can play hide-and-seek.

It may say: "Let's dance!"

Artists see a masterpiece.

It's an ever-changing,
always open, everyone
welcome art gallery.

27

Wherever we are, we share the same sky.

It is the roof over our heads.

Picture the sky. How do you feel?